FLASH OF LOVE

"WHISPERS OF AFFECTION A LOVE REFLECTION"

PRATYUSHA KANUMETTA

To all those who believe in the magic of unspoken connections,
This book is for you—the dreamers who find love in the smallest
gestures, the believers who see destiny in a flash of light, and the
romantics who cherish the stories written by fate.

To my viewers and supporters, your unwavering encouragement
and belief in this journey have been my guiding light. Thank you
for allowing these characters and their love to find a place in your
hearts.

And to love itself—its simplicity, its depth, and its ability to shine
even in the darkest moments—this story is my humble ode to you

To my beloved parents,
The architects of my dreams and the unwavering pillars of my strength. Your guidance, patience, and unconditional love have been the light that has illuminated my path. This story carries whispers of your faith in me, woven into every word.

To my dear brothers,
The silent warriors of my journey, whose camaraderie and subtle yet profound support have been my shield and inspiration. Your belief in my ideas and your quiet encouragement have made this story a reality.

This book, Flash of Love, is not just a tale of romance and resilience—it's a testament to the bonds that shape us, the love that empowers us, and the family that grounds us.

With all my heart,

Pratyusha Kanumetta

Contents

Preface

Love, they say, is a force that transcends time, space, and even life itself. For Adhya, this sentiment could not be more true. What began as an innocent romance with her beloved Avirbhav soon spiraled into a chilling mystery, testing the very boundaries of love and courage. Little did she know that beneath the surface of their blossoming relationship lurked a restless soul—a painter girl whose unfinished mission bound her to Avirbhav in ways neither of them could comprehend.

At first, Adhya saw the strange occurrences as signs of trouble in her relationship, a threat to the love she cherished so deeply. But as the truth unraveled, it became clear that she wasn't merely protecting her bond with Avirbhav; she was standing between him and a force beyond the natural world. Through fear and uncertainty, Adhya's devotion never wavered. Her determination to free the soul trapped between worlds would lead her down a path fraught with peril, but also one that revealed the true power of love.

In this tale, The Flash of Love, love becomes both a weapon and a shield as Adhya fights to protect Avirbhav, herself, and the memory of a love that had been lost to time. Her journey is not just about setting a soul at peace; it is a testament to the lengths we go for those we love, and the unshakable belief that love can overcome even the most haunting of forces.

This is a story of courage, of secrets long buried, and of a love that flashes brightly even in the darkest moments.

In the journey of love, we often find ourselves leaning on the pillars of strength that family provides. Flash of Love is not just a tale of two souls discovering each other; it is also a celebration of the love, support, and warmth of family bonds that light up the darkest corners of our hearts.

Adhya's parents, though protective, hold an unspoken trust in her choices. Their subtle encouragement becomes the wind beneath her wings, teaching her to soar while staying grounded. Her mother's tender smiles and her father's steady guidance act as silent affirmations, allowing her to find her own path.

Avirbhav's family is no less extraordinary. His younger brother, with his infectious energy, becomes a confidant and a co-conspirator in crafting moments that spark joy. His unwavering faith in Avirbhav's dreams reflects the bond only siblings share—a bond built on shared laughter, whispered secrets, and unshakeable belief in each other.

Together, these familial ties enrich Adhya and Avirbhav's story, reminding us that love thrives not just between two hearts but within a circle of unwavering support. This book is dedicated to those families who silently and steadfastly hold our hands, helping us navigate through life's storms and celebrations.

May Flash of Love inspire you to cherish the love that begins at home and extends beyond, like the flash of light breaking through the clouds—a sign of hope, connection, and God's silent blessings.

Foreword

Dear Readers,

It is with immense joy and gratitude that I welcome you to Flash of Love. This story, crafted with love, is a tribute to the unspoken emotions, fleeting moments, and hidden symbols that define the purity of a bond. Through the pages of this book, I hope to take you on a journey where love transcends words, communicated instead through the glimmer of light and the quiet power of connection.

To all the dreamers who find magic in the smallest gestures, to the romantics who believe in divine signs, and to the brave souls who fight against the odds for love—this story is for you.

I owe my deepest thanks to the unwavering support of family, friends, and mentors who encouraged me to bring this tale to life. A heartfelt thank you goes out to the readers who continue to inspire authors like me by believing in the power of storytelling.

May this book remind you of the beauty in vulnerability, the strength in perseverance, and the brilliance of light in even the darkest corners.

Love is a journey often marked by unspoken gestures, hidden sacrifices, and the delicate interplay of trust and understanding. While this story unfolds the tender and resilient bond between Avirbhav and Adhya, it is also a celebration of the unwavering support that surrounds them—their family.

Behind every step of courage that Adhya takes, her parents' silent prayers and quiet strength echo. Though they have built a protective cocoon around her, their love is the compass that eventually allows her to navigate the stormy seas of her emotions. Similarly, Avirbhav's daring spirit is shaped by the foundation of encouragement from his family, particularly his brother, who often acts as his confidant and partner in mischief.

In the pages that follow, you will discover not just the romantic chemistry between two souls but also the subtle influences of a family's belief in their loved ones' happiness. Adhya's parents, though initially hesitant, become the gentle breeze steering her toward her dreams. Avirbhav's brother, with his blend of wit and wisdom, serves as a constant reminder that love is not a solitary venture but one shared by those who stand by us.

This story is an ode to the intricate dynamics of family, where love transcends its usual confines and blossoms into a tapestry woven by parents' dreams and siblings' camaraderie. Together, they form the invisible threads binding Avirbhav and Adhya's tale—a story of love that shines brighter because of the light others reflect onto it.

Flash of Love is a reminder that sometimes, the greatest flashes of light don't come from thunderous storms but from the steady glow of loved ones standing by.

With love and gratitude,
Pratyusha Kanumetta

Acknowledgements

With immense gratitude, I dedicate this book, Flash of Love, to all the dreamers, believers, and lovers of stories that touch the heart.

To my readers, your support and passion breathe life into my words. Thank you for embracing this tale of hidden emotions, unspoken confessions, and the extraordinary bond of Avirbhav and Adhya. Your enthusiasm inspires me to craft stories that resonate deeply.

To my friends and family, your encouragement has been my guiding light. Thank you for believing in my vision, even when it was just a spark of an idea.

To those who kept me going during late-night writing marathons—whether it was through a kind word, a hot cup of coffee, or a gentle reminder to keep moving forward—your love has made this journey truly unforgettable.

Lastly, to the unseen magic that binds hearts and lights the darkest paths, this story is a humble tribute. May it remind us all that love, in its purest form, will always find a way.

ACKNOWLEDGEMENTS

I express my deepest gratitude to my parents, whose unwavering love and support have been the bedrock of my journey. Their endless encouragement, gentle guidance, and belief in my dreams have been my greatest strength. From the smallest moments of inspiration to the monumental milestones, their presence has been a constant source of motivation. This book, in many ways, reflects the values and resilience they have instilled in me.

To my brothers, my pillars of strength and my greatest cheerleaders—I cannot thank you enough. Your boundless energy, words of encouragement, and occasional playful banter kept me grounded and inspired throughout this journey. You've been my sounding boards, my critics, and my strongest supporters, and I am eternally grateful for your faith in me.

Together, you all have been my lighthouse in the storm, guiding me back to my path whenever I drifted. This book, "Flash of Love," would not have been possible without your belief in my vision and your endless encouragement. Thank you for walking this journey with me and for being the heart of every word penned in this story.

With love and light,
Pratyusha Kanumetta

Prologue

Prologue: Flash of Love

In a quiet town shrouded by the whispers of tradition and the echoes of dreams, the lives of two souls intertwined, their bond as unique as the flash of a light in the dark.

Adhya, a gentle yet spirited miniature artist, spent her days bringing the tiniest of details to life on her canvas. Behind her soft demeanor lay a fierce heart that longed to soar beyond the walls her parents had built around her. Her world was one of colors, secrets, and silent dreams of freedom.

Avirbhav, a gifted guitarist with a charm as electrifying as the tunes he played, was the boy next door who carried his passion like a flame. Despite his rebellious streak and zest for life, his heart knew where it truly belonged. His love for Adhya, though unspoken, burned bright like a thunderstorm that once changed everything.

In the heart of their story was Rupshi, Adhya's best friend and her partner in countless adventures. Rupshi, with her quick wit and fiery spirit, stood as the bridge between Adhya's sheltered world and the vast realm of possibilities beyond it.

Their lives took a dramatic turn when fate drew them to a forgotten museum, a cursed painting, and a night that revealed truths they had long buried. As Adhya and Avirbhav navigated the labyrinth of their hearts and the challenges of a strict, watchful society, their love found its unique language—a flash of light that spoke volumes when words failed.

Through thunderstorms, whispered secrets, and moments that teetered between the real and the surreal, their journey unfolded, bound by love, tested by fate, and illuminated by the flash that became their bond.

In the darkened corners of their world, the light of their love burned steady, a beacon that dared to defy the odds.

Rupshi had always been the spark in any room, the kind of person whose laughter could light up even the darkest corners of a room. With her boldness and wit, she was the friend everyone turned to for advice, or simply to share a moment of joy. But beneath her confident exterior was a heart that had long been hidden, one that yearned for something real but feared the vulnerability it would bring.

Her best friend, Adhya, was the opposite—quiet, reserved, with a heart full of untold stories. Rupshi often found herself acting as Adhya's protector, guiding her through the challenges of life, especially the complexities of her budding romance with Avirbhav. But while Rupshi was always there for Adhya, she kept her own desires locked away.

ONE

ADHYA IS ALL SET FOR CONFESSION

<u>Adhya is all set for confession</u>

Adhya paced nervously in Rupshi's living room, holding a crumpled piece of paper. Her heart raced as she rehearsed the poem she'd written for Avirbhav, each word a confession of the feelings she had bottled up for so long.

"I-I... love the way you... no, that sounds silly," she muttered, shaking her head. "I love the way you smile, the way you make even the ordinary seem extraordinary. Agh, why is this so hard?"

Rupshi, her best friend lounging on the sofa with a smirk, teased, "You know, you could just tell him, 'I love you, idiot!' and call it a day."

Adhya flushed deep red, lowering her gaze. "It's not that easy, Rupshi. Every time I think of him, I just—" She buried her face in her hands. "I blush like an idiot!"

Rupshi laughed, tossing a pillow at her. "You're adorable. Just breathe, okay? You'll be fine."

Before Adhya could respond, her phone rang. She fumbled to answer it, her palms suddenly clammy. "Hello?"

"Adhya, it's Swati, from the hospital," the voice on the other end said urgently. "I don't know how to tell you this, but... Avirbhav just came in with blood-stained hands."

Adhya's face drained of color. "W-what? Blood-stained? Is he hurt? What happened?" Her heart pounded, and her knees felt weak.

"I'm not sure of all the details yet, but you need to come to the hospital right now," Swati said gently, sensing her panic.

The phone slipped from Adhya's trembling hands as she stared at Rupshi in disbelief. "Avirbhav... he's hurt. He's at the hospital."

Rupshi jumped up, grabbing Adhya's arm. "Come on, let's go."

At the hospital, Adhya practically ran through the hallways, her breath coming in shallow gasps. Her mind raced with a thousand horrific scenarios, each one worse than the last. What had happened? Why was he hurt?

Rupshi was right beside her, trying to calm her down, but Adhya's anxiety drowned out everything. The moment she spotted Avirbhav sitting on a hospital bench, his hands bandaged but still slightly red from the blood, her legs gave out beneath her.

"Avirbhav!" she called weakly, her vision blurring as she staggered toward him.

Avirbhav's eyes widened, and he rushed forward just in time to catch her before she collapsed. "Adhya, hey, hey! I got you."

Adhya barely heard him as her head spun. But when she regained her senses a few moments later, lying in a hospital bed, she immediately sat up, anger flaring within her. "What the hell,

Avirbhav?! What happened? Why were your hands—"

Avirbhav shot a look at Rupshi, a mischievous smirk curling his lips. "Oh, that? Well... I cut my hands. I couldn't take it anymore, Adhya. You never listen when I try to convince you how much I love you, so..."

Adhya blinked, her mind racing. "W-what are you saying?"

Rupshi, catching on to his teasing, rolled her eyes. "Oh boy, here we go."

Avirbhav continued, feigning sorrow as he held his bandaged hands out dramatically. "I couldn't handle it, Adhya. It was too much. You, not believing me. So I thought... maybe if I hurt myself—"

Before he could finish, Adhya slapped him hard across the face. "You idiot! What kind of nonsense is that? How could you be so... so stupid?!"

Avirbhav, rubbing his cheek with an amused grin, said, "Okay, I deserved that."

Rupshi burst into laughter while Adhya fumed. "This isn't funny!"

Just then, a nurse approached with a kind smile. "Excuse me, miss. The child Avirbhav brought in is stable now. His condition has improved significantly. You can see him if you'd like."

Adhya blinked, confused. "Child? What... what's she talking about?"

Avirbhav, looking sheepish now, rubbed the back of his neck. "Okay, okay. Before you yell at me again, let me explain. I didn't harm myself, alright? I saw a kid in an accident on the way here, and I rushed him to the hospital. His condition was critical, and I got his blood on my hands while carrying him."

Adhya's anger slowly melted into relief. "So... you're not hurt?"

"Nope, not even a scratch," Avirbhav said, smiling softly. "But you'll only get the full story if you promise to calm down."

Adhya's lip trembled as she felt the wave of emotions crashing over her—relief, anger, embarrassment, and love all mixed together. She sighed heavily, resting her forehead against his chest. "You really scared me, you know that?"

Avirbhav chuckled, gently brushing her hair out of her face. "I know. I'm sorry. But... I also now know how much you care."

Adhya looked up at him, her blush returning in full force. "You already knew that, didn't you?"

Avirbhav's eyes softened, his tone playful yet sincere. "Yeah... but it's nice to hear it without words too.

TWO
AVIRBHAV'S TOUCHING GIFT

Adhya, still recovering from the hospital scene, walks alongside Rupshi and Avirbhav as they approach his house. The sun is setting, casting a soft orange glow on the street, which seems to calm the tension in the air.

Avirbhav unlocks the door, stepping in first and gesturing for them to follow. "Come in, you both," he says with a hint of playfulness. "I've got something to show you."

Adhya, trying to stay composed, gives him a cautious glance. "Something to show me ?"

Rupshi, catching on to the teasing tone, elbows Adhya lightly. "Careful, Adhya, he might be planning to pull a prank."

Avirbhav chuckles as they walk into the living room, his hand brushing through his messy hair. "No pranks today, promise." He looks back at Adhya, his eyes softening. "Just something I've been working on."

He moves to a small table, carefully picking up a miniature heart crafted out of delicate clay, its edges detailed intricately with fine lines. Some dried clay still stains his fingers. He holds it out to her with a proud smile.

"This... this is what stained my hands earlier. I was finishing it for you," Avirbhav says gently, watching her reaction. "Wanted to make sure it was perfect."

Adhya's eyes widen in surprise, her heart racing at the sight. "You were making this for me?" She reaches out, carefully taking the miniature heart from his hands, her fingers grazing his for a brief moment. The detail, the effort—it leaves her momentarily speechless.

Rupshi, standing behind her, peers over her shoulder. "Wow, Avirbhav! That's some dedication!" She nudges Adhya again, grinning. "You must be really special, huh?"

Blushing, Adhya avoids Rupshi's playful gaze and looks back at Avirbhav. "You didn't have to go this far... but it's beautiful," she says softly. "Thank you."

Avirbhav smirks. "Well, I had to show you somehow that my hands weren't stained with blood. You almost gave me a heart attack back at the hospital, you know."

Adhya lets out a small laugh, relieved. "I'm sorry about that." She pauses, her smile softening. "Actually, I was thinking... maybe we could meet tomorrow? There's this Peers cafe I've been wanting to try. How about it?"

Avirbhav raises an eyebrow, surprised. "You... want to meet me tomorrow?"

"Yes." Adhya nods, her confidence growing. "Just us. At the cafe."

Rupshi gasps dramatically, breaking the moment. "Wait, wait! Before anything else, I want something in return for being the best wing-woman ever."

Adhya rolls her eyes playfully. "What now, Rupshi?"

Rupshi grins mischievously. "You both owe me the story of how you first met. Promise me you'll narrate it to me after your meetup tomorrow!"

Avirbhav chuckles, exchanging a glance with Adhya. "You really want to hear that story?"

"Yes, and I want all the details!" Rupshi insists, folding her arms and raising her eyebrows expectantly.

Adhya sighs, giving in with a smile. "Alright, alright, we promise. Tomorrow after the cafe, you'll get the full story."

Avirbhav steps closer to Adhya, his eyes locking with hers. "Looks like we have a lot to talk about tomorrow."

Adhya's heart flutters, and she manages a nod, her voice barely above a whisper. "Yes... we do."

THREE

RUPSHI DEMANDS FOR THE LOVE STORY

In a cozy, dimly lit café, Rupshi sat across from Adhya and Avirbhav, her excitement bubbling over as she asked them to narrate their recent adventure. The ambiance was filled with the light hum of chatter, but her focus was fully on the lovebirds.

"Come on! Spill the tea! How did it all begin?" Rupshi teased, her eyes wide with curiosity.

Avirbhav glanced at Adhya with a soft smile, his hand resting lightly on hers under the table. "You want to start?" he asked her.

Adhya giggled, tucking a loose strand of hair behind her ear. "Fine, fine. So, we were both invited to this really old museum, one that almost no one gets to see. I was there for the art—miniatures, of course—and Avirbhav, well, the guitarist in him wanted to explore the historic musical instruments."

"Sounds like the perfect set-up!" Rupshi grinned, leaning in closer.

"Yeah, perfect... until we got locked in," Avirbhav added with a chuckle.

"The power went out, and it was just the two of us in this giant, creepy museum. No lights, no sound... only the two of us sitting in the corner, waiting for someone to rescue us," Adhya continued, her voice soft but full of hidden excitement. She recalled how the silence between them was more than just the absence of sound—it was charged with a tension that neither had acknowledged yet.

Rupshi gasped dramatically. "Oh no! What did you guys do?"

"Well, we sat there gossiping," Avirbhav said, casting a mischievous glance at Adhya. "It started innocently enough, just talking about random things. But then it became... different. We started talking about stuff that was, you know... more personal."

Adhya blushed, looking away for a moment. "It was romantic, in a way. Sitting in the dark, just the two of us... sharing thoughts we never had before."

Rupshi raised an eyebrow. "And then?"

Adhya's eyes twinkled as she leaned in. "Well, I suddenly felt something crawl on my feet. I freaked out."

Avirbhav took over, a playful glint in his eye. "Being the hero I am, I decided to light up the place." He pulled out an imaginary bottle from his jacket, mimicking the moment. "I had my favorite perfume with me, and there was an old painting just lying around."

"You didn't!" Rupshi gasped, clasping her hands together in disbelief.

"Oh, I did," he laughed, "I tore a piece of the painting and used my perfume to light it up like a makeshift torch."

"But here's the weird part," Adhya interrupted, lowering her voice as if sharing a secret. "We both felt something... strange. Like there was this presence with us. The air got heavy, and it felt like we weren't alone."

"Creepy! What did you do?" Rupshi asked, wide-eyed.

"We ignored it," Avirbhav shrugged. "You know, just your typical haunted museum stuff."

"But it didn't feel normal," Adhya whispered. "Still, we decided to leave as soon as the door opened."

Avirbhav leaned back, his smile softening. "By the time we got out, it was raining. We were stuck there a little longer. I wanted to say something... something important."

Rupshi's eyes flicked between them. "What did you say?"

Avirbhav's eyes softened as he looked at Adhya. "I told her, 'You know, I feel like this place, this night... it's special. Like maybe things happen for a reason.'" His voice dropped to a whisper, and Rupshi could sense the weight of his unspoken words.

Adhya smiled shyly, her fingers lightly touching the table. "And I left... before he could say more. My dad was expecting me home, and I was already late. But when I ran out into the storm, it felt like the universe was giving us a sign."

"A sign?" Rupshi tilted her head, intrigued.

Adhya nodded. "There was this huge thunderclap, and it reminded me of the first time we both realized we liked each other... during that thunderstorm months ago. I took it as a divine approval of whatever was happening between us indeed it was the Flash of Love .

Avirbhav smirked. "She ran off before I could even tell her properly."

Rupshi clapped her hands together. "So romantic!

Avirbhav's face became more serious. "After she left, I talked to the museum authority about it. Turns out, it was an abandoned painting from a girl... and they warned me about strange things happening ever since they got it. But I didn't care. I bought it anyway."

Rupshi's eyes widened. "Why?"

Avirbhav smiled softly, his eyes meeting Adhya's. "Because I wanted to give her something to remember that night by. It felt... right. Like it would be a memory for life."

Adhya looked down, her smile warm and full of affection. The thunderstorm may have given them divine approval, but this painting would forever remind them of the night their love truly began to blossom.

FOUR

FLASHES GUIDING THE LOVE

Adhya sits by her window, staring out at the quiet evening sky, her thoughts lost in the memory of her and Avirbhav's shared secret. The sound of her parents' voices in the background reminds her of the strict expectations they have for her—rules she's expected to follow without question. They don't know about Avirbhav, and they wouldn't approve if they did. The love between them is a delicate blossom, carefully protected from the harsh winds of the world she lives in.

As the evening darkens, she sees a familiar flash of bike lights from down the road—Avirbhav's secret signal. It's their code, a silent conversation that speaks volumes. Adhya's heart races, remembering the stormy night when they first confessed their love for each other, the thunder and lightning feeling like a divine sign.

Adhya's Thoughts:"That night... it was like the heavens gave us their blessing. Every time I see those lights, it feels like our own private language."

parents won't notice her quiet presence for a moment. From his bike down the street, Avirbhav sees her and flashes the light again—two quick bursts, their signal for "I'm here." Adhya smiles softly, her heart swelling with warmth.

A few days later, Avirbhav carefully plans something simple but meaningful. He knows Adhya's favourite chocolate—one she can rarely get because she's always under her parents' watchful eyes. That evening, while riding past her house, he subtly places the small chocolate in her mailbox, timing it perfectly so she finds it before anyone else does.

When Adhya discovers the little surprise later that night, her heart skips a beat. It's not just the chocolate—it's the effort, the thought behind it. She clutches it to her chest, knowing that even in her confined world, Avirbhav is always thinking of her.

Adhya: (whispering to herself) "He's always finding a way to make me feel special... even when we can't be together."

One late night, Adhya's phone lights up with a message. It's from Avirbhav.

Avirbhav: "Can you come to the balcony? Just for a minute."

Adhya carefully sneaks to her balcony, heart pounding with the thrill of their secret. She sees Avirbhav waiting in the shadows, his bike parked nearby, the headlights off to avoid suspicion. He grins when he sees her.

Avirbhav: (teasing) "You're getting good at sneaking around."

Adhya: (laughing softly) "I've had practice. My parents are still in the living room though, so we can't talk long."

Avirbhav flashes the bike lights—just once, softly—a reminder of their secret code.

Avirbhav: "Remember the storm that night? I still can't believe how perfectly the thunder struck when we... well, you know."

Adhya smiles, her cheeks flushing at the memory.

Adhya: "I still think it was a sign from God. It felt so right, like everything was falling into place for us."

Avirbhav: (playfully) "If that's the case, then I guess the universe is on our side, huh?"

Their conversation is brief but filled with warmth. As Avirbhav leaves, he flashes the lights again—a soft goodbye that means "I'm with you, always."

One afternoon, knowing Adhya's love for the rain, Avirbhav waits until her parents are out. When the first raindrops fall, he sends a message.

Avirbhav: "Check your balcony."

Adhya steps out and sees Avirbhav standing below, holding a small bouquet of wildflowers—drenched but smiling as the rain falls around him. He looks up, flashing that familiar grin, knowing how much she loves the little moments of joy.

Avirbhav: "I couldn't let you miss out on this one!"

Adhya giggles from her balcony, shaking her head at his soaked appearance but feeling overwhelmed by the sweetness of his gesture.

Adhya: (calling down) "You're crazy, you know that?"

Avirbhav: (laughing) "For you? Always!"

A few weeks later, another storm rolls in—thunder rumbles in the distance, and the sky grows dark with heavy clouds. Adhya is sitting in her room, waiting for the familiar flash of Avirbhav's bike lights, knowing he'll find a way to reach her despite the storm.

And just as expected, through the curtains, she sees it—two quick flashes, their code. Her heart races, and she sneaks out to the balcony, the rain starting to fall in sheets.

Avirbhav is there, standing with his bike parked nearby, his helmet off and soaked by the rain, but his face bright with a smile.

Avirbhav: "Looks like we've got another thunderstorm. Think it's a sign again?"

Adhya can't help but laugh, feeling that familiar warmth bloom inside her. The thunder rumbles overhead, and she looks at Avirbhav, feeling the connection between them grow even stronger.

Adhya: (smiling) "It always is. Every time."

They stand there, the storm swirling around them, the flash of lightning overhead feeling like another blessing—a reminder that, despite the challenges, they've found something worth protecting. And no matter how strict her world is, Avirbhav will always find a way to nurture their love, even in the smallest, most precious ways.

Avirbhav knows that Adhya loves books—especially the ones she borrows from her local library. One afternoon, knowing which book she's going to borrow next, he sneaks a small note inside the pages. It's a simple message, but one that makes Adhya's heart melt when she finds it.

The note reads:

"For every chapter you turn, remember I'm here, waiting for our next page together."

When Adhya finds the note later that evening, curled up in her room with the book, she can't help but smile. She immediately sends him a message.

Adhya: "You know you're ruining books for me, right? Now all I'll be thinking about is you!"

Avirbhav: "Mission accomplished."

Knowing Adhya's parents monitor most of her online activity, Avirbhav finds a way to make their conversations even more personal—through music. He curates a secret playlist of songs that remind him of her and sends it to her with a coded message, disguised as a generic playlist so her parents wouldn't suspect anything.

When Adhya listens to it later that night, she hears songs that remind her of their moments together—songs that make her smile, cry, and feel connected to him, even when they can't speak.

One of the songs ends with a whispered voice recording:

Avirbhav: "For every beat, I'm thinking of you. Can't wait to see you smile again."

Adhya's heart flutters, knowing that even in something as simple as a playlist, he finds a way to be close to her.

Avirbhav knows Adhya's favorite flowers are jasmine—delicate and fragrant, but something her parents would never think to bring her. One night, when he knows her parents are asleep, he sneaks over to her house and carefully leaves a small bunch of jasmine flowers tied with a soft ribbon just outside her bedroom window.

He doesn't text her right away, wanting her to find them herself in the morning.

The next day, Adhya wakes up to the sweet scent of jasmine drifting through her window. When she sees the flowers, her heart swells with happiness. She knows it's from Avirbhav, without him even needing to say it. She carefully tucks one of the flowers into her diary as a keepsake.

Later, she sends him a picture of the flowers with a message:

Adhya: "How do you always know the perfect thing to do?"

Avirbhav: "I listen. That's the secret."

Knowing Adhya's parents are strict about her phone usage, Avirbhav gets creative. He starts sending her random "innocent" messages—like funny memes, images of nature, or even a random picture of his bike. But hidden within each image is a subtle message only Adhya can decode.

For example, one image of a sunset over a field has the words:

"Look closely—there's something beautiful hidden in every corner, just like you in my life."

Adhya becomes an expert at finding these hidden messages, loving how Avirbhav always makes her day feel brighter without raising suspicion.

Avirbhav knows Adhya can't wear anything that might give away their relationship. So, he creates something special for her—a simple ribbon bracelet. He carefully ties it together with a small charm, nothing flashy, but meaningful.

One day, while they manage to sneak a few moments together at a quiet corner in the park, he slips the bracelet into her hand.

Avirbhav: "It's nothing fancy, but I wanted you to have something small... something that's just ours."

Adhya smiles, her fingers tracing the soft ribbon as she slips it onto her wrist. It's small enough that her parents won't notice, but every time she looks at it, she'll think of him.

Adhya: (whispering) "I'll never take it off."

Knowing how much Adhya loves the rain, Avirbhav starts writing her letters every time there's a heavy downpour. He hides these letters in a spot they both know—behind a loose brick in a garden wall near her house. The letters are sweet, filled with love and little jokes.

One day, during a rainy afternoon, Adhya sneaks out to find one of the letters. When she opens it, she finds this:

"I know you're smiling right now, reading this in the rain. Every raindrop is a little piece of me, falling for you."

Adhya clutches the letter to her chest, feeling overwhelmed by how much thought Avirbhav puts into even the smallest gestures. Even in the rain, she feels his presence, as if the storm is wrapping them both in a secret embrace.

All these small, meaningful efforts show how Avirbhav nurtures their blossoming love in a world that doesn't always allow them to be together. Each action is a reminder to Adhya that, no matter how confined her environment may be, their love finds a way to grow through every little gesture.

FIVE

THE FIRST FIGHT

It was one of those rare days when Avirbhav and Adhya had planned to meet at their usual spot—a quiet park with an old bench under a large tree. The sun filtered through the leaves, casting a soft dappled light, but today, the atmosphere between them felt tense, the calm of the place contrasting sharply with the frustration in their hearts.

Avirbhav sat on the bench, arms crossed, his foot tapping anxiously on the ground. Adhya stood in front of him, her arms folded defensively, biting her lip as she stared at him.

"You know, Avirbhav, I just don't get why you can't see it from my perspective," Adhya began, her voice strained but controlled. "Every time you brush off my concerns about your career plans, it feels like you don't care what I think."

Avirbhav sighed, rubbing his temples. "It's not about that, Adhya. It's just... I have my own timeline, okay? I can't just jump into something serious because you think it's the right time."

"I'm not asking you to change your whole life for me!" Adhya shot back, her voice rising in frustration. "But if we're serious about each other, you need to start thinking about the future. You can't keep living day to day like this!"

Avirbhav stood up abruptly, the tension between them spiking as he took a step closer. "Do you even hear yourself? You're making it sound like I don't care about us! Just because I'm not making huge decisions right now doesn't mean I'm not invested in this relationship."

Adhya's eyes flashed with hurt, but she held her ground. "That's not what I'm saying, and you know it. It's about planning, about thinking long-term. Do you even know where you see us in five years?"

Avirbhav's frustration boiled over, his voice rising as he retorted, "Why does everything have to be about 'five years from now'? Can't we just enjoy what we have without constantly overthinking the future?"

Adhya clenched her fists, her emotions getting the better of her. "Because I need to know! I need to feel like we're moving forward, that we're not just stuck in the same place, pretending everything will work out without any effort!"

They stood there, both breathing heavily, the weight of the argument hanging between them. A long silence followed, the only sound the faint rustling of leaves in the breeze.

Finally, Avirbhav exhaled, running a hand through his hair in frustration. His voice was quieter now, filled with an underlying vulnerability. "I get it, Adhya. You want something solid, something you can hold on to. But I'm scared too, okay? Scared of making the wrong choices, of rushing into things and messing them up."

Adhya's expression softened slightly, the anger giving way to something more tender. "I'm not asking for perfection, Avirbhav. I'm just asking for honesty. If we're going to make this work, I need to know you're willing to fight for it too."

Avirbhav looked at her, the tension in his body easing as he stepped closer, his voice barely above a whisper. "I am fighting for it, Adhya. Every day. I just... sometimes, I don't know how to show it."

Adhya took a deep breath, her defenses slowly crumbling. "Then show me. Be there for me, not just today, but tomorrow and the day after. I need to feel like we're in this together."

He reached out, gently taking her hand, the warmth of his touch surprising her. "I'm not perfect. But I promise, I'm not going anywhere. I want us to work, even if we fight like this sometimes."

For a moment, they simply stood there, the intensity of the argument dissolving as they locked eyes. Something shifted between them—something deeper than words could express.

Adhya blinked, a small, vulnerable smile forming on her lips. "You know, I wasn't expecting us to have our first big fight over something like this."

Avirbhav chuckled softly, shaking his head. "Neither was I. But I guess it shows we care too much to just let things slide."

She nodded, stepping closer, their fingers entwining naturally. "I care more than I realized."

Avirbhav leaned in, his forehead gently resting against hers, his voice soft but sure. "I think that's what makes us stronger. Even when we fight, we still end up here—together."

Adhya closed her eyes, feeling his presence so close, her heart calming as she whispered, "I love you, Avirbhav."

He smiled, his hand cupping her cheek as he tilted her chin up to look at him. "I love you too, Adhya. More than words."

And just like that, their first fight transformed into something far more meaningful—an unspoken bond, forged in the fire of their emotions but tempered with the realization that they were stronger together than apart.

SIX

AVIRBHAV HAS A SURPRISE FOR ADHYA

A cool evening breeze filtered through the open window of Rupshi's room Adhya stood by a small desk in Rupshi's house where she occasionally rests when Adhya is alone at home , carefully working on one of her miniature art pieces. The soft glow of her lamp casts long shadows on the walls, and she was lost in her thoughts when a gentle knock on the door broke her focus.

"Come in," she called absentmindedly, assuming it was Rupshi .

To her surprise, it was Avirbhav, standing at the doorway with a large, covered frame in his hands. His usual playful smirk was replaced with something softer, almost hesitant.

"Avirbhav?" she asked, her eyebrows knitting together in curiosity. "What are you doing here with that?"

Avirbhav stepped in, leaning the frame carefully against the wall. "I wanted to give you something," he said, his voice quieter than usual. "Something to remember... you know, that night."

Adhya's heart skipped a beat. "The night at the museum?"

He nodded, gesturing to the frame. "Go on. Open it."

With tentative hands, Adhya removed the cloth covering, revealing the painting underneath. Her breath caught as her eyes fell on the image—the same girl in royal attire they had seen in the museum, her expression both regal and haunting. The very painting from which Avirbhav had torn a piece during their strange encounter in the dark.

Her fingers brushed lightly over the painting's surface, tracing the intricate details of the girl's gown. "This is... the one from that night," she whispered, a flood of memories rushing back—the eerie darkness, their whispered conversations, the brief, charged moment when Avirbhav had torn a piece to create light.

Avirbhav stood behind her now, his voice gentle. "I know we didn't think much of it then, but... that night was special. And when I saw this painting again, I knew it had to be yours."

Adhya turned around, her eyes wide, filled with a mix of wonder and disbelief. "But... you bought it? They actually sold this to you?"

Avirbhav grinned, shrugging. "Yeah, with a fair bit of convincing. They said it's cursed or something, but I didn't care. It's ours now... and I thought, maybe, it could remind us of how things started between us."

SEVEN

ADHYA SENSES STRONG PARANORMAL PRESENCE

Adhya , excited by the gift her boyfriend has given her, hangs the large, beautifully framed painting. It's a portrait of a young woman with a hauntingly serene expression, her eyes almost too lifelike. She feels an eerie connection to the painting but brushes it off as artistic admiration. That night, as she prepares for bed, she hears a soft, rhythmic tapping. Following the sound, she finds it coming from the room where she placed the painting. The eyes in the portrait seem to follow her as she moves around the room. Unnerved but determined, she boldly approaches the painting, tapping it back as if to challenge whatever might be lurking within. Adhya too tired with all the perceptions that ran in her head falls fast asleep.

As the days go on, Adhya begins to hear whispers—soft, unintelligible, but persistent. They emanate from the walls of her home, growing louder near the painting. The whispers turn into mournful cries when she's alone at night. However, the girl, with a bravery that surprises even herself, confronts the noise, speaking back to it, demanding to know what it wants. The cries suddenly stop, replaced by the sound of a brush moving across a canvas. When she checks the painting, she finds that the figure's expression has changed—now, the woman looks terrified.

It was late at night, and the soft glow of moonlight barely illuminated her space. The house was eerily quiet, save for the occasional creak of the wooden floorboards. She sat on her bed, gazing at the painting, lost in thought, when she suddenly heard a faint, rhythmic tapping.

The sound seemed to echo through the walls, and Adhya froze, listening intently. It was coming from the direction of the painting. Her heart began to race, a cold shiver running down her spine. She brushed it off as her imagination, convincing herself that it was just the wind or an old house settling. But then, the tapping grew louder, more insistent, almost as if someone — or something — was knocking from the inside of the canvas.

Nervously, Adhya walked closer to the painting, her breath shallow. As she neared it, the room temperature dropped suddenly, and she could see her breath fogging the air. The painting seemed different now, darker, and the figure of the woman in the background appeared slightly shifted. Was it her mind playing tricks on her, or had the woman in the painting moved?

Adhya stepped back, but as she turned to leave, a soft, whispering voice echoed around her, chilling her to the bone. It was faint at first, like a breeze carrying a message she couldn't quite grasp. She whipped her head around, looking for the source, but there was no one. The house was empty. The voice grew louder, more distinct. It was pleading, desperate. "Help me..."

Suddenly, the lights flickered. In the brief moments of darkness, she could swear she saw shadows dart across the room, closer and closer. When the lights came back on, everything seemed in place, except for one terrifying detail — the woman in the painting now stared directly at her, her eyes wide open and filled with sorrow.

Panicked, Adhya backed away, her legs shaking. She stumbled toward the door, but as her hand touched the doorknob, a force pulled her back into the room. Her screams echoed through the house, but they were swallowed by the oppressive silence that followed. The painting's frame rattled violently on the wall, and the whispering voice returned, louder now. It filled the room with an overwhelming presence, suffocating her senses.

With her heart racing and fear tightening her chest, Adhya felt something cold brush against her skin, like icy fingers tracing the outline of her arm. She spun around, but nothing was there. The tapping resumed, this time from behind her, relentless and closer than ever.

In a desperate move, she grabbed her phone to call Avirbhav, but before she could press the call button, the phone flickered and died, the screen going black. She felt utterly alone, trapped with whatever entity had come through the painting.

Then, as if to confirm her worst fears, the painting began to drip. A dark, viscous liquid seeped from the corners, staining the wall beneath it. Adhya's chest tightened, her breaths shallow, as the ghostly figure in the painting seemed to reach out toward her, its eyes filled with sorrowful rage.

Just as she thought she would be consumed by the fear, the room was lit up by a flash of light — a bike light, blinking through her window. Avirbhav's familiar signal cut through the oppressive darkness, reminding her that he was nearby, trying to communicate with her.

Summoning every ounce of courage, she bolted toward the window, the painting's presence still looming ominously behind her. As she flung open the window to signal back, the haunting whispers receded, leaving her standing there, breathless and shaken, wondering if she had just imagined it all — or if the painting held secrets far darker than either of them realized.

EIGHT

ADHYA'S SHOCKING REVELATION

cozy café they frequent. As she approaches their usual table, she sees Avirbhav laughing and talking animatedly with a beautiful woman who looks ethereal, her presence almost otherworldly. The woman is dressed in a flowing, vintage-style dress, her hair cascading in loose waves. Adhya's heart drops, assuming that Avirbhav has found someone new. Trying to hide her hurt, she joins them, but neither Avirbhav nor the woman acknowledges her presence. Avirbhav continues to talk, seemingly to himself, while the woman smiles softly, her gaze occasionally shifting to Adhya with a knowing look. Confused and hurt, Adhya leaves the café abruptly, thinking Avirbhav is having an emotional affair with this mysterious woman.

Over the next few days, Adhya notices Avirbhav spending more and more time "alone," but she often catches glimpses of the woman beside him. In the park, at the movies, even during their intimate moments, the woman is always there, sometimes standing close, sometimes watching from a distance. Adhya's confusion deepens into jealousy and despair as she feels increasingly shut out of Avirbhav's life. Every time she tries to talk to him about the woman, Avirbhav looks at her like she's lost her mind, insisting that no one else is there. Adhya begins to doubt her own sanity, wondering if she's imagining things. The weight of the situation plunges her into depression, as she feels like she's losing Avirbhav to someone she can't even touch or compete with.

Adhya's depression deepens as she grapples with the reality of what she has discovered. She tries to distance herself from Avirbhav , feeling an overwhelming sense of helplessness and guilt. One evening, Avirbhav invites her over for dinner, trying to rekindle their relationship. As they sit across from each other, the lady suddenly appears from nowhere , standing behind Avirbhav, her expression one of intense longing. Adhya watches in horror as the woman leans in close to Avirbhav, whispering something into his ear that she can't hear. Avirbhav suddenly smiles, as if comforted by the presence, completely unaware of what is happening , he himself indulged in remembering few previous incidents .

Adhya , her heart breaking, excuses herself and leaves in tears, unable to bear this sight . " Adhya wait" pleaded a voice from behind Adhya turned back to find her best friend Rupshi . She hugged her tight desperately and started weeping bitterly, Rupshi managed to console her, " Avirbhav rung me up this evening and said I'm going for a date with my angry bird nothing but a few gulps of ice cream can chill her up if possible do click few pictures of us together , my princess really likes natural candids of us together" " this is what Avirbhav said to me" explained Rupshi . Adhya relaxed for a moment and started rethinking the special bond they shared together, " Adhya lets just take a look at the pictures I have just clicked" said Rusphi and then they both started looking at the pictures together , " Wait a minute" said Adhya in a tone of confusion " Any problem Adhya ?" questioned Rupshi " How come only we both are in the pictures and not that lady ?" asked Adhya " Lady ? which lady I didn't happened to notice anyone in the couple of minutes you were with him Adhya ?" said Rupshi totally puzzled " That's impossible Rupshi , how come you didn't notice her ? entire time she was so glued to Avirbhav" replied Adhya completely messed up . " I swear I haven't seen anyone Adhya" confirmed Rupshi. Entirely out of mind they both leave to their respective places.

Once Adhya gets back home , she lays down quietly on the couch trying to join up the parts of the entire scenario that is created , she was about to fall asleep when suddenly there is a knock at the door , Adhya opens up the door to her neighbour aunt " Adhya, looks like you are too tired , well you needed few old newspapers for home cleanup , here they are !" , saying this she handed over the old newspapers and left for home . Adhya too tired to place them in the store room kept them on the table with a minimal paper weight to prevent it from flying over . As she was trying to settle back to relax one of the newspaper fell on the floor just behind her bed ; Adhya picked up the newspaper carelessly and was about to put it on the table . " Wait ! what !!!" Adhya cried out in utmost shock when she noticed the picture of the girl she saw on the newspaper , below it was written Upsha 1992-2020 . Adhya was taken aback when she learned that it's the spirit of a dead painter that's been moving with her love .

Determined to free both Avirbhav and herself from this torment, Adhya delves into the history of the painter. Adhya quickly rings up the number given below

She discovers that the woman was a talented artist who died under tragic circumstances, her soul forever tethered to her unfinished work. Armed with this knowledge, Adhya instead of employing methods to cast off the spirit , chooses to be kind enough to help the soul attain peace .

NINE

ADHYA TRIES TO JOIN THE DOTS

Adhya sat at her desk with her friend Meera whom she invited over , papers scattered around, as she stared at her laptop screen, scrolling through countless records. The room was dimly lit, save for the soft glow of the screen and a faint beam of moonlight seeping through the window. The quiet hum of the ceiling fan was the only sound as she sifted through her research on Upsha, the dead painter whose ghost she had encountered through her boyfriend.

Adhya's friend, Meera, sat across from her, helping her with the search. "Upsha's story is so tragic," Meera said, pushing a strand of hair behind her ear. "She was engaged but died before she could give her fiancé a gift. A painting, I think."

Adhya paused, her eyes widening. "What kind of painting?" she asked, her heart pounding in her chest.

Meera clicked on another record, skimming through it. "It says here... she had painted his sister in royal attire as a wedding gift. But the painting was never delivered. Upsha passed away before she could give it to him."

Adhya's mind raced as memories of a particular painting in her home flashed before her eyes. Her boyfriend had gifted her a beautiful, intricate portrait of a woman in regal clothing not too long ago. She stood abruptly, her chair scraping the floor. "Wait... that painting... the one he gave me. It's her!" she whispered, panic and realization mixing in her voice.

Meera looked confused. "What do you mean?"

"I have it, Meera. The painting Upsha made for her fiancé... it's in my house. It's the one he gave me," Adhya said breathlessly, her thoughts spinning. How had it ended up with her? And why had her boyfriend, of all people, gifted it to her?

Meera's eyes widened. "Are you serious? That's... eerie."

Adhya nodded, still reeling from the realization. "I need to find out more," she muttered, her determination intensifying. She had to know Upsha's story.

After days of searching, Adhya finally managed to obtain Upsha's diary from a distant relative who had kept it all these years. Sitting on her bed, she opened the old, faded journal, the scent of aged paper filling the air. Her fingers trembled slightly as she began reading the first few pages.

The entries were full of life, filled with Upsha's love for painting and her passion for capturing the beauty of the world around her.

."March 22: Today, I painted another portrait of him... my love. He looks so dashing in his navy coat, standing tall as if he's about to conquer the world. I can't wait to show him all these paintings... I've drawn him in every attire I imagined he'd wear on our wedding day. Oh, how I dream of the day we stand before our friends and family, as husband and wife. The roses around us, the scent of flowers filling the air... Our home, nestled amidst a garden filled with red and white roses... Our little paradise.".

Adhya's eyes softened as she imagined Upsha painting, lost in her love for her fiancé. The next entry made her heart ache.

."April 10: I can't wait to give him the final painting... it's not of him this time, but of his sister, the one he cherishes so dearly. I've painted her in royal attire, like the queen she is to him. I hope he loves it. This will be my wedding gift to him... but first, I need to finish the last few details.".

Adhya gasped softly, tears welling up in her eyes. Upsha had never gotten the chance to gift the painting. The diary entries grew more emotional as she neared the end.

."April 27: I feel strange, weaker than before. But I must finish the painting... I must give it to him. The roses in our garden will bloom soon. I can already hear the music we will play together, me on the violin and him on the piano. It will be perfect. Our dream home will be filled with music, love, and laughter.".

Adhya closed the diary, overwhelmed. Upsha's life, her love, and her dreams were so vividly captured within these pages. She could feel Upsha's hope, her excitement for the future, and her deep love for the man she never got to marry.

Tears trickled down **Adhya's** cheeks as she whispered, "You never got to give him the painting, Upsha... but somehow, it found its way to me. And I promise, I'll make sure your fiancé knows about it."

She knew now that she had a responsibility. Upsha's story needed to be completed, her gift finally delivered.

TEN

DIGGING INTO HER DIARY

Adhya, still clutching Upsha's diary, couldn't help but wonder how such a passionate, talented young woman had her life cut short. Her fingers delicately traced the aged pages as she flipped to the next entry, hoping the answer would be revealed.

."May 1: I've been feeling ill these past few days. It started as a slight fever, but it's become worse. I've been coughing and feeling dizzy more often. I promised myself I would finish the painting, but I barely have the strength to hold my brush. He came to visit today, and I tried to hide how bad I was feeling. I don't want him to worry... but I can see the concern in his eyes. I just need a little more time... just a little more.".

Adhya's heart sank. The sickness that plagued Upsha was becoming more apparent in the following entries. She read on.

."May 4: I can barely breathe. The fever won't go away, and I'm too weak to get out of bed. I know something is wrong, terribly wrong. My love visited again today, and I couldn't hide it from him this time. He held my hand, promising me I'd get better. But I saw it in his eyes... he's scared. And so am I. I just want to see him one more time, healthy and happy, and give him the painting. But I fear... I fear I might not have the chance.".

Adhya's eyes blurred with tears. She could feel Upsha's fear, her desperation. The entries were growing shorter, the handwriting shakier, as if Upsha had struggled to even hold the pen.

."May 8: The doctor says it's pneumonia. He's given me medicine, but... I know my body. I can feel myself slipping away. I don't have much time left. I haven't finished the painting. I don't want to leave him... I don't want to leave him alone.".

Adhya's chest tightened as she turned to the final entry, written with great effort.

."May 10: I can't finish it... I can't finish the painting. I wanted to give it to him, to show him how much I love him, how much I care for his family. But I'm so tired... I'm so cold. I pray he finds it one day and knows it was meant for him. My love, I will always be with you, in every flower, every rose in the garden, every song that plays on our piano and violin. I will love you forever... even if I'm not there.".

Adhya wiped away the tears streaming down her face. Upsha had died of pneumonia, her illness taking her before she could fulfil her final wish. She never finished the painting, never gave her fiancé the gift she had poured her heart into.

Adhya closed the diary gently, overwhelmed by the sorrow of Upsha's untold story. "She died... waiting," she whispered, her voice thick with emotion. "She didn't get to say goodbye."

But as Adhya glanced at the portrait on her wall—the painting of the woman in royal attire that her boyfriend had gifted her—she knew that in some strange, mysterious way, Upsha's wish had been fulfilled. The painting had survived, even if Upsha hadn't.

ELEVEN

FETCHING THE MAN OF THE HOUR

Adhya's curiosity about Upsha's fiancé grew stronger as she read through the diary. She couldn't shake the question: .What happened to the man Upsha loved so deeply?. Determined to find the answer, she dug deeper into historical records, using every resource she could access, from archives to local history forums. Finally, she found a lead—a small collection of letters written by Upsha's fiancé, a man named Tarak, stored in an old museum's digital archive.

One of the letters caught her attention. It was dated only a few weeks after Upsha's death.

..Letter from Tarak to a Friend :..

."I hardly know where to begin. Every day since Upsha's passing has felt like a slow, agonizing dream. I still wake up expecting her to be there, her soft voice, her laughter filling the room. But then I remember... she's gone. Pneumonia, they said. It took her so quickly.".

."I cannot describe the pain, the emptiness that has taken hold of my heart. She was my light, my muse, my future. Without her, I feel lost. I visit her grave every day, but even that does not bring me peace. I feel as though part of me was buried with her.".

."I don't know if I'll ever be able to move on from this grief. How does one live when the future they dreamed of, the life they built in their mind, is snatched away so cruelly? Upsha and I had plans—plans for a house filled with music and roses. I can still hear her talking about our rose garden, how she would play her violin in the evenings while I played the piano. I see it all so clearly, but I will never touch that reality.".

."I loved her more than words can describe, and though she is gone, I feel her with me every moment. Perhaps someday I will find the strength to finish the painting or to let it go. But for now, it sits there, just like my heart—unfinished, forever longing for what was lost.".

Adhya read the letter over and over, her heart breaking for Tarak. He had been devastated by Upsha's death, unable to move on from the life they had imagined together. His grief was palpable, and he had held onto the unfinished painting, unable to complete it or let it go.

Adhya leaned back in her chair, staring at the painting on her wall. She could see it now with fresh eyes. It wasn't just a beautiful piece of art. It was the last thread of a love story that never had a chance to flourish. Tarak had mourned Upsha for the rest of his life, never truly moving on from the grief of losing her. He never married or found solace. Instead, he devoted his remaining years to preserving her memory, refusing to let go of the love they had shared.

Whispering softly, Adhya said, "He never forgot you, Upsha. He carried you with him until the end."

Upsha's story was one of love, loss, and the unfinished dreams of a future that never came to pass. But now, in some strange way, Adhya felt like she had become part of that story too. The painting, once a symbol of tragedy, had found a new home—a home where it was cherished and loved, just as Upsha had once intended.

TWELVE
ADHYA APPROACHES SHANAYA FOR HELP

Adhya knocked softly on the door of Shanaya's office. It was late, and the faint hum of the wind outside mixed with the distant sound of footsteps from the university's empty corridors. Inside, Shanaya, a PhD holder in paranormal research, sat surrounded by books, charts, and old relics from her studies. She looked up as Adhya entered, concern etched on her face.

"Adhya? It's late. You look stressed. What's going on?" Shanaya asked, putting aside the notes she was reviewing.

Adhya sighed deeply, sitting across from Shanaya. "Shanaya... I need your help. It's about a ghost, a soul that hasn't found peace yet."

Shanaya raised an eyebrow, immediately intrigued. "A ghost? Who? Where? Start from the beginning."

Adhya ran a hand through her hair, struggling to find the right words. "You remember the painting my boyfriend gifted me a few months ago? I've been researching it, and I discovered it's connected to a painter named Upsha, who died before she could give it to her fiancé. Upsha's soul... she hasn't moved on."

Shanaya leaned forward, her eyes narrowing. "How do you know she hasn't found peace? What makes you think her soul is still lingering?"

Adhya bit her lip, hesitating before replying. "I've seen her. Around my boyfriend. I don't know why, but she's always... there. She doesn't appear to me, but I sense her. And sometimes, I catch glimpses of her—just around him."

Shanaya frowned thoughtfully. "So, the ghost is fixated on your boyfriend? That's strange. There must be something about him that's keeping her attached. Ghosts typically don't just follow people without a reason. There must be a connection."

"That's what's bothering me," Adhya said, her voice trembling slightly. "My boyfriend has no idea. He's not connected to Upsha in any way that I know of. But her spirit won't leave him alone. It's like she's drawn to him."

Shanaya tapped her fingers on the desk, deep in thought. "Tell me, Adhya, does your boyfriend have anything in common with Upsha's fiancé? Anything at all? Sometimes spirits get attracted to shared elements—similarities in their birth stars, physical traits, even something as simple as scent."

Adhya's eyes widened as she considered the possibilities. "Birth stars... hair... clothes... No, I don't think there's anything like that. But—wait!" she exclaimed suddenly. "There was something! We were at a museum when he first saw the painting. He had this new perfume he was trying, and he sprayed it near the painting before we left. It was an old habit of his to wear perfume around expensive things."

Shanaya's gaze sharpened. "Perfume? That might be it. Ghosts, especially ones that haven't found peace, can be incredibly sensitive to scents. Some perfumes, especially certain ingredients, can evoke strong memories or emotions from their past. It's possible Upsha's spirit latched onto him because the perfume triggered something from her life."

Adhya leaned back, shocked by the realization. "So you're saying... Upsha's spirit was attracted to my boyfriend because of his perfume? But... why would that happen?"

Shanaya explained, "Perfumes are powerful. For the living, they trigger memories. For the dead, they can act as magnets. It's possible Upsha's fiancé wore a similar scent, or maybe the perfume reminded her of something she associated with love, comfort, or familiarity. It's not uncommon for spirits to be drawn to specific stimuli like this. The perfume might have acted as a bridge between Upsha's lingering emotions and your boyfriend."

Adhya nodded slowly, absorbing Shanaya's explanation. "That makes sense... In Upsha's diary, she always talked about her fiancé, about their love, and how she wanted to build a life with him. I think the perfume... it connected her to my boyfriend, and she mistook him for the person she loved. That's why she's still here."

Shanaya stood up, pacing slowly. "Exactly. If her soul is wandering and hasn't found peace, she may be clinging to your boyfriend as a surrogate for her lost love. It's not intentional, but it's like a gravitational pull. Now, the real question is—how do we help her move on?"

Adhya looked at Shanaya, her voice soft but determined. "That's what I need your help with. How do I help her rest in peace?"

Shanaya stopped pacing, her face serious. "We'll need to recreate the emotional closure she never had. She's trapped in a loop, still waiting to give that painting to her fiancé. If we can find a way to complete that connection—whether it's through acknowledging her love or guiding her towards the realization that she's free—we might be able to help her find peace."

Adhya's heart raced as hope flickered in her chest. "So, you think it's possible?"

Shanaya nodded firmly. "It's possible, Adhya. But it's going to take some work. We'll need to figure out the exact trigger—whether it's the perfume or something deeper—and then guide her toward her final resolution."

Adhya smiled, feeling a weight lift off her shoulders. "Thank you, Shanaya. I don't know what I would've done without you."

Shanaya smiled back, though her eyes were still focused and calculating. "Don't thank me yet. We've got a lot of work to do. But if we can help Upsha, we'll be helping more than just her. You'll be setting your boyfriend free from her lingering presence too."

Adhya nodded, ready to begin the next step of her journey to bring peace to Upsha's soul.

THIRTEEN

LOVE BIRDS REUNITE

Adhya stood outside Avirbhav's house, the evening air crisp and cool against her skin. She had been pacing for what felt like hours, trying to muster the courage to face him after their argument. Things had gotten tense between them over the last few days, and she hated how distant they had become. But tonight, she was determined to fix things. They had a way of communicating, a secret little code they used to share—flashing the light of her phone to send silent messages of love. She hoped it would work again.

She took a deep breath, raising her phone. With a playful smile, she flashed the light once, then twice. It was their signal—a throwback to the early days when they'd secretly meet under the streetlights, sharing stolen moments in the strict environment they both navigated. The light had always meant, .I'm here, I love you..

At first, nothing happened. Adhya bit her lip, wondering if she'd lost him for good. But then, after a few seconds, the front window flickered. The light flashed back at her—once, then twice.

Her heart skipped a beat.

Avirbhav stepped out onto the porch, his expression guarded but softened by the hint of a smile. "You're still using that, huh?"

he said, his voice teasing but carrying a note of warmth.

Adhya chuckled softly, taking a step closer. "It worked before, didn't it?" she said, shrugging lightly, her eyes twinkling with mischief. "I thought I'd try it again."

Avirbhav folded his arms across his chest, clearly still upset but no longer as distant. "You know we can't just fix everything with a flashlight, right?" he said, though his voice lacked the sharp edge it had earlier.

Adhya took another step toward him, her smile widening. "Maybe not... but it's a start. Remember when we used to do this every time we wanted to meet without anyone knowing?" She flashed her light again, three quick bursts. "And what does .this. mean?"

Avirbhav couldn't help the small laugh that escaped him. ".I miss you,." he said, his voice softening. He sighed and ran a hand through his hair, his eyes finally meeting hers. "But it's not that simple, Adhya."

She nodded, moving closer, until she was standing right in front of him. "I know it's not. I know I messed up, and I've been distant with everything going on. But I've missed us. I've missed .you.."

Avirbhav glanced away, clearly torn. "You always get wrapped up in things, Adhya. You shut me out. It's like you disappear into your world, and I'm left standing here, waiting."

Adhya's eyes filled with regret, her hand reaching for his gently. "I'm sorry, Avirbhav. I never meant to push you away. I get caught up in things, but... I need you. You're the one who always brings me back to reality. I love you."

He stared at her for a long moment, then exhaled slowly. "You know... I love you too. That's why it hurts so much when you pull away."

Adhya smiled softly, her thumb brushing over his hand. "Then let's not pull away anymore," she said, her voice filled with hope. "Let's go back to how we were before... when it was just you and me, our secret codes, our silly games."

Avirbhav smirked, his defenses finally breaking down. "You think we can just pick up from where we left off? Like old times?"

Adhya's playful grin returned. "Why not? We can always start with this." She held up her phone again and flashed the light in a familiar pattern, the one that meant, .I love you..

Avirbhav's smile widened as he reached into his pocket and pulled out his own phone, flashing his light back—.I love you too..

In that moment, all the tension, all the distance between them seemed to dissolve. Avirbhav pulled her into a tight embrace, resting his chin on her head. "I missed you," he whispered softly.

Adhya buried her face in his chest, feeling the warmth and comfort of being back in his arms. "I missed you more."

After reconciling with Avirbhav, Adhya's life seemed to return to normal, but deep down, she knew that something still lingered—Upsha's spirit had not yet found peace. Though she had patched things up with her boyfriend, she couldn't shake the feeling that Upsha's presence was still near, waiting for closure.

Over the next few days, Adhya's dreams became increasingly vivid. Each night, she would see Upsha, sometimes standing in a vast rose garden, sometimes playing the violin in a grand home that Adhya recognized from Upsha's diary. It was as if Upsha was trying to tell her something—showing her the life she had imagined with her fiancé, the future that had been taken away from her.

One morning, Adhya awoke with a start, a realization striking her like a bolt of lightning. She had been so focused on helping Upsha move on that she had forgotten the most crucial detail—Upsha had never been able to give her fiancé the painting she had worked so hard on. That unfinished gesture was the key to helping Upsha find peace.

Determined, Adhya met with Shanaya once again. "I've been having these dreams," Adhya explained as they sat across from each other in Shanaya's cluttered office. "Upsha is showing me the life she never had. I think she's trying to communicate with me."

Shanaya nodded thoughtfully. "That makes sense. Spirits often use dreams to convey messages when they can't reach us directly. Upsha's probably trying to show you what she never got to experience—her home, her love, her music."

Adhya leaned forward, her eyes intense. "But it's more than that. She never got to give her fiancé the painting. I think that's why she's still here. I have to finish what she started."

Shanaya smiled softly. "That might be exactly what Upsha needs. But are you sure you're ready to take on this responsibility? You'll have to create the closure that Upsha never had."

Adhya nodded, her resolve firm. "I have to. For her. And for Avirbhav. This has affected us both. I won't be at peace until she is."

The next few days were a whirlwind. Adhya worked tirelessly on the painting, her hand guided by what felt like more than just her own intuition. With every brushstroke, she could feel Upsha's presence, as though the painter herself was standing over her shoulder, gently guiding her movements. She recreated the woman in royal attire, finishing the delicate details that had been left incomplete for over a century.

When the painting was finally done, Adhya felt a strange sense of calm wash over her. It was as if the weight of Upsha's unfinished story had been lifted. But there was still one final step: she had to return the painting to its rightful place.

FOURTEEN

UPSHA'S SOUL RESTS IN PEACE

It's late evening, and the soft glow of streetlights filters through the trees of the park. Adhya and Shanaya stand in a secluded area, a prearranged spot with two mirrors discreetly positioned at an angle. They're planning something that will finally bring peace to Upsha's restless spirit—without Avirbhav finding out.

..Shanaya:.. (whispering) ."Are you sure Avirbhav doesn't suspect anything? We need to be extra careful. If he finds out we've been doing this behind his back, he might try to interfere. Upsha's spirit could sense his involvement and resist.".

..Adhya:.. (nodding) ."I've been keeping him distracted, don't worry. He has no idea. We've come too far to mess this up now.". She adjusts one of the mirrors. ."So, tell me again... how does binding the spirit between the two mirrors work?".

..Shanaya:.. ."Spirits can get trapped between reflective surfaces. When we position two mirrors facing each other, it creates a sort of dimensional loop. Once the spirit is caught between them, it's easier to control or communicate with. The goal is to intrigue Upsha's spirit long enough to draw her here. The moment she steps in, we bind her.".

..Adhya:.. ."And that's where the perfume comes in. Upsha always wore this scent, so I'll use it to get her attention.". She pulls out a bottle of an old, floral fragrance. ."I'll speak to her, make her linger. Meanwhile, I'll keep checking the paranormal device for her presence.".

Shanaya nods, the tension in her eyes clear, but she trusts Adhya. The plan is set.

Adhya walks toward the open space between the mirrors. The air feels cooler, almost charged. She sprays a light mist of the perfume, watching the paranormal device flicker. It detects the spirit's presence.

Adhya: (softly, into the air) ."Upsha, I know you're here.". She sees a faint shimmer in the air, a sign Upsha is listening. ."There's something I want to tell you. I know about your painting... your final work... the one for Nayan.".

The shimmer intensifies, drawing closer to her. Upsha's spirit is curious.

..Adhya:.. (gently) ."It's not too late, Upsha. Nayan... he still loves you. He never forgot you, even after all this time. Don't you want him to see your last gift to him? It's beautiful... the one you never got to deliver.".

The device hums louder, confirming the spirit's movements. Adhya carefully steps back, leading Upsha toward the space between the two mirrors. She can feel the energy tightening, knowing she's almost got her.

Adhya:"Come with me, Upsha. I'll take you to Nayan... just step right here." She gestures subtly toward the spot between the mirrors.

The shimmer floats closer until it's trapped between the reflective surfaces. The moment Upsha's spirit is bound, the atmosphere shifts, and the mirrors glimmer faintly, containing her presence.

Avirbhav arrives at the scene with Nayan . One's face filled with confusion and the later's face with hope .Both look at Adhya, unsure of what to expect. " You asked me to pick this guitarist from the studio without telling me anything else ?" inquired Avirbhav . "Yes and just see what follows Avi" said Adhya

Adhya: (smiling softly) "Nayan, there's something I've been keeping for you." She hands him the painting, Upsha's final masterpiece. "This is from Upsha. It's the piece she wanted to give you before..."

As Nayan takes the painting into his hands, his eyes well up with tears. He gently traces the strokes of the artwork, overwhelmed with emotion. Avirbhav tries to listen attentively and draw conclusions.

Nayan: (voice cracking) "This... this is her work. I never thought I'd see it." He looks at Adhya. "Will she be happy now? Is she finally at peace?"

..Adhya:.. (smiling warmly) ."Yes, she is. She's watching over you even now. She's always been with you, in ways you didn't see. And she'll continue to be a part of you. That's why I made this.". She hands him a miniature sculpture she crafted—a delicate representation of all Upsha and Nayan had dreamed of together the beautiful house amidst the garden of roses the dream balcony with their favourite violin and piano and all other details instinctively sculpted as per the information led by Upsha's diary

.

Nayan looks at the tiny sculpture, the memories flooding back. He holds it close.

..Nayan:.. ."Upsha... she always wanted this. It's like she's still here with me.".

..Adhya:.. (softly) ."She is.". She glances at the mirrors, where Upsha's spirit watches silently. ."Would you like to see her one last time?".

Nayan nods, tears in his eyes, unable to speak. Adhya activates the paranormal device, adjusting its settings to allow Nayan to see Upsha's spirit. Slowly, the shimmer forms into the faint outline of Upsha, her face soft and radiant.

..Nayan:.. (whispering) ."Upsha...?".

Upsha's spirit smiles gently, her eyes full of love. She lifts a hand, as though saying goodbye.

..Upsha:.. (softly, though only Adhya can hear) ."Thank you...".

With that, her spirit begins to dissolve into the light, flowing upward and away, her soul finally at peace.

The air is still, yet filled with a subtle warmth as the last remnants of Upsha's spirit fade into the light. Her final goodbye has left a profound quiet over the space, like the closing of an old, lingering chapter. Nayan wipes the tears from his eyes, clutching the painting and miniature sculpture close to his chest. He turns to Adhya, his voice shaking with gratitude.

Nayan: (softly) "I... I don't know how to thank you. Both of you. Upsha's at peace because of you." He glances at Avirbhav, who's standing a few steps away, still absorbing everything that's unfolded. "I can finally move on, knowing she's free."

Avirbhav, who has just learned the full truth, stands silently, staring at the spot where Upsha's spirit had once been bound between the mirrors. His face is a mixture of emotions—relief, confusion, frustration, and perhaps even a trace of sadness. He shifts his gaze to Adhya, searching for words but finding none.

Adhya, sensing his inner turmoil, steps closer to him.

Adhya: (gently) "Avirbhav... I didn't tell you everything because I knew you'd take it too personally. You're so sensitive to these things, to the spirits. I needed to make sure Upsha's soul could rest without your emotions interfering."

Avirbhav: (voice low, uncertain) "So you kept me in the dark?" His eyes flicker with a mix of hurt and bewilderment. "All this time, you were doing this behind my back?"

Adhya reaches out, placing a reassuring hand on his arm. Her voice is calm, filled with understanding.

Adhya: "Yes. I know you're upset, but you have to understand—I didn't want to risk anything. Upsha needed closure, and I needed to make sure she got it. If you were involved from the start, it could've made things harder for both her and you."

Avirbhav exhales, running a hand through his hair. He's overwhelmed with conflicting emotions—part of him wants to be angry, but another part knows Adhya is right. He feels a strange emptiness, knowing that Upsha's spirit is gone, but also relief that she's finally at peace. The researcher in him wants answers, but the human part of him feels a deep sense of loss.

Avirbhav: (after a pause) "I don't know what to feel right now." He glances at Adhya, his eyes searching hers. "I've been chasing this... this presence for so long, and now it's gone. I should be relieved, right?"

Adhya nods, understanding his confusion.

Adhya: "You're allowed to feel conflicted, Avirbhav. It's okay. You cared deeply about Upsha's spirit, even if you didn't know her personally. But this is what she needed. Letting go is hard, but it's necessary sometimes."

Avirbhav looks down, the weight of her words settling in. He feels a tear form at the corner of his eye but quickly wipes it away, not wanting to show how deeply affected he is. Adhya notices, but she doesn't comment on it. She knows him too well.

Avirbhav: (quietly) "I guess I just... I wasn't ready."

Adhya: "I know. That's why I didn't tell you until now. I needed you to focus on moving forward, not holding onto the past. And now, Upsha's story has come to an end. Nayan can finally live with peace, and so can you."

At that moment, Nayan steps forward, his face still wet with tears but filled with gratitude.

Nayan: "Avirbhav, Adhya... I don't know how to thank you both enough. You've given me something I never thought I'd have—closure. Upsha meant everything to me, and now I can finally feel her love again without the weight of sadness."

He takes a deep breath, looking at both of them with sincerity. Nayan: "You've done something incredible, not just for her, but for me. I'll never forget this."

Avirbhav, though still processing his emotions, nods quietly, acknowledging Nayan's words. Shanaya, standing beside them, places a comforting hand on Nayan's shoulder.

Shanaya: (smiling) "You don't have to thank us, Nayan. It was the right thing to do—for everyone. Upsha's finally where she belongs, and that's all that matters."

As the sun dips lower, casting a golden hue across the park, the four of them—Avirbhav, Adhya, Shanaya, and Nayan—stand together in a quiet moment of reflection. The weight of the journey they've been on together begins to lift, replaced by a sense of immense gratitude.

Avirbhav: (breaking the silence) "I guess... I should be grateful too. For both of you." He glances at Adhya, his tone softer now. "You did something I couldn't, Adhya. You set her free."

Adhya smiles gently, her heart swelling with relief that Avirbhav finally understands.

Adhya: "We all played a part. Upsha's peace was always the goal, and now we can all move on."

Shanaya looks at both of them with a warm smile, her voice filled with quiet pride.

Shanaya: "We helped a soul find its way home. That's something to be proud of."

The group stands together in silence for a few moments, each of them reflecting on the events that have unfolded. There's a shared understanding between them, a bond formed from the emotional journey they've been through together. A deep sense of gratitude fills the air—not just for what they've accomplished, but for each other.

As they begin to walk away from the park, the soft glow of the sunset on their backs, Avirbhav takes a deep breath, feeling a strange but peaceful weight lift from his heart. For the first time in a long while, he feels lighter, as though he's finally let go of something he's been holding onto for far too long.

As the light fades, Nayan stands in silence, holding the painting and miniature art close. He feels a sense of closure, of finality, knowing that Upsha is finally free. And when they area all set to leave there was a heavy rain followed by a flash of thunderstorm , Adhya and Avirbhav smiled at each other and said to themselves God never misses even though we do . Avirbhav arms around Nayan and whispers him Upsha loved capturing your every special moment in her paintings right , so does she now. Bro remember everytime it rains its Upsha capturing you from the heaven and its her way of communicating with you through the flashes of love.

About Author

Pratyusha Kanumetta a recently qualified Cost and Management Accountant and Masters in Commerce , is an enthusiastic explorer of the vivid fanatsies of story telling . Love fights all odds is what we have heard but is it strong enough to fight with a paranormal force sticked to its goal ? Well , this book prooves you that love is the greatest power in the universe . Enjoy delving into the lives of a young talented couple trapped in mysterious paranormal circumstances , their ways to deal with it sheltering their blossomed love .*"Love is never just one story. It's a mosaic of moments, emotions, and people, each adding a unique shade to the picture. In Flash of Love, I wanted to capture not just the obvious romantic moments, but the quiet, unseen connections that build the foundation of our deepest relationships.Through Adhya and Avirbhav, I explored the magic that exists in small, shared experiences—the flash of a bike light, the touch of a hand, the unspoken bond that transcends words. But it's also about the unsung heroes—the friends, the silent witnesses, the ones who may not always get the spotlight, but who shape the path of love in their own subtle ways.In the end, Flash of Love isn't just about two people falling in love; it's about the way love affects everyone around us and how it shapes us into who we are meant to be. I hope readers find something of themselves in these pages, and perhaps, like the flash of a light in the dark, feel that love is always just within reach, waiting to be discovered in the most unexpected ways."*Pratyusha Kanumetta